For Rebecca and Joe

Paperback ISBN 0 340 65350 7

A catalogue record for this book is available from the British Library.
First edition published 1996

8 10 9 7

Published by Hodder Children's Books, a division of
Hodder Headline Limited, 338 Euston Road, London NW1 3BH
Printed in Hong Kong

SCARED of a BEAR

Hilda Offen

A division of Hodder Headline Limited

“Please come and play,” said Katie.
“I’m having a tea party.”

“Your house is too small,” said Gran.
“We wouldn’t fit in,” said Mum.
“And we’re all far too busy,” said Tom.

Katie stamped her foot.
"Then I shall go to the forest," she said,
"and play on my own."

"No! NO!" they cried. "Don't you dare!
There are bears in the forest -
They're as tall as this! And as wide as that!
They're mean! They're fierce! They're scary!"

But Katie wasn't bothered.
Katie didn't care.

She went into the forest
and there she met…

a BEAR!

“Bears aren’t scary at all,” said Katie.
“My family were wrong.
Bears are small!
Bears are cuddly!
Bears are really good fun!”

“Come to tea,” said Katie.

And off they went.

They were nearly home when they met Tom.
"Look, Tom," called Katie.
"Bears aren't fierce. They're friendly."

But Tom shouted "Help!"
and ran away.

Next they met Gran.
“You were wrong, Gran,” said Katie.
“Bears are smaller than me.”

"Oh my goodness!" gasped Gran.
She jumped over a wall and ran away too.

Then they met Mum.
"Bears aren't scary, Mum," said Katie.
"Meet my new friend."

But Mum dropped all the pegs
and started to shake like a jelly.

"BEHIND YOU!" cried Mum, Gran and Tom.
Then Katie turned - and she looked -
and she blinked! For there stood
the little bear's mother!

"RUN!" shouted Mum.
So they started to run.
And the BIG, FIERCE, ANGRY bear
ran after them.

“We’ll be safe indoors,” puffed Mum.

But the doorway was high -
it was high, it was wide -
and the big bear easily got inside.
"Keep running," called Katie,
"I know where to hide."

They ran to her little house;
and they pushed and they squeezed
and they all squashed in.

But the mother bear was much too
big to get through the door.
She growled and she growled and
she prowled round the house.

"Quick! Quick! Think of something!
What shall we do?"
Katie opened the window
and pushed the little bear through.

"Now you're here," said Katie,
"you can all stay for tea."

And the big bear
and the little bear
went away.